CONTENTS

THE MYSTERY LAKES

Lakes are large areas of water that are entirely surrounded by land. 'Loch' is a Scottish word that means 'lake'. Lakes can be over 213 metres deep, and these great depths can make them very mysterious.

LOCH NESS, SCOTLAND

Loch Ness is the deepest lake in Great Britain. It is in the Great Glen, an ancient fault that cuts the mountainous Highlands in the north of Scotland in two. The fault has been active for 400 million years. The last earthquake along it was in 1901.

Abriachan

Drumnadrochit

Urquhart Bay

N

W ← → E

S

Inverfarigaig

LOCH NESS

Length: 38 kilometres
Width: 1.49 kilometres
Sea level: 15.8 metres above
Average depth: 132 metres
Maximum depth: 229 metre

Foyers

Invermoriston

Loch Ness is a popular tourist attraction in the Highlands.

Fort Augustus

LAKE CHAMPLAIN, UNITED STATES OF AMERICA

Lake Champlain is one of the most historically rich areas of water in North America. It was used as a travelling route by Native Americans. It drains into the Richelieu and St. Lawrence rivers to the north in Canada, and is fed by Lake George and the Hudson River to the south in New York State.

Length: 193 kilometres
Width: 19 kilometres
Sea level: 32 metres above
Average depth: 21 metres
Maximum depth: 230 metres

Lake Champlain is an important source of drinking water.

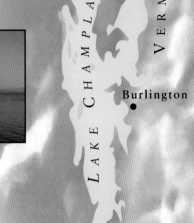

LAKE ERIE, UNITED STATES OF AMERICA

Lake Erie is the eleventh largest lake in the world. It is the fourth largest of the five Great Lakes, which are located between the United States and Canada.

Lake Erie is the shallowest and most biologically diverse of the Great Lakes.

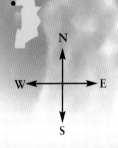

Length: 388 kilometres
Width: 91 kilometres
Sea level: 914 km above
Average depth: 18 metres
Maximum depth: 64 metres

MONSTER ORIGINS

For thousands of years, large, seemingly bottomless inland waters, like Loch Ness, have inspired a sense of mystery and given rise to ancient legends.

MYTHS AND LEGENDS

As well as the legend of the monster at Loch Ness there is the legend of the Kelpie. This spirit was said to live in and around Loch Ness. It appeared as a saddled horse waiting by the lake shore. If a tired traveller climbed onto its back, it would leap headlong into the waters to drown them.

The legendary Kelpie, or water horse, was said to lurk by Scottish lakes.

MONSTER HOTSPOTS

In addition to Loch Ness, and Lakes Erie and Champlain in the United States, monsters have been reported in Canada, China, and Norway. The world's deepest lake, Lake Baikal in Siberia, is also thought to be home to a monster. If these creatures really do exist, what are they?

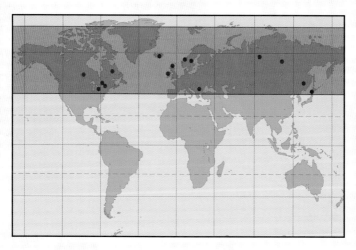

Some cryptozoologists think that all reported sightings of lake monsters occur on the same band of latitude. They call this area the 'Boreal Forest Belt' but have yet to prove their theory.

UNDISCOVERED CREATURES

Could these lake creatures be an undiscovered species of animal? Some people certainly think it's possible. The giant panda, the Kodiac bear, and the mega-mouth shark were all unknown to science until the last century.

Were ancient stories of sea serpents really the sightings of unknown types of animal?

Another example of a recently discovered animal is the coelacanth. This species of fish was thought to have been extinct for over 70 million years, until one was found alive in 1938. Could other prehistoric animals have survived without us knowing? If so, these so-called lake monsters could swim the deep without requiring a supernatural explanation for their existence.

The giant squid was thought to be mythical until scientists found one in 1997 that had recently died.

THE LOCH NESS MONSTER

THE WATERS OF LOCH NESS, SCOTLAND, 565 A.D. A GROUP OF MEN CROSSING THE LOCH WITNESS A DISTURBANCE IN THE WATER...

THERE'S A MAN IN TROUBLE!

GAAAAAGH! HELP ME!

QUICK! HAUL HIM IN.

WE'RE TOO LATE – HE'S GONE.

HE DIDN'T DROWN, THOUGH. LOOK AT THAT WOUND!

BY THE SAINTS! WHAT KIND OF CREATURE COULD HAVE MADE SUCH A LARGE BITE?

THE BEAST, WHICH HAD SEEMED ABOUT TO EAT POOR LUGNE...

LORD, HAVE MERCY!

...SUDDENLY VANISHES, AS IF PULLED BACK BY ROPES.

SWOOOOOSH!

THE STORY DOESN'T END THERE, HOWEVER.

LOCAL LEGEND SAYS THAT IN THE SUMMER OF 1527, A TERRIBLE BEAST EMERGED FROM THE LOCH TO RAMPAGE OVER THE SURROUNDING LAND. IT KNOCKED DOWN TREES AND KILLED THREE MEN BEFORE SINKING BACK BENEATH THE WATERS.

ANOTHER TERRIFYING SIGHTING OCCURRED IN 1879, WHEN A GROUP OF CHILDREN SAW A STRANGE CREATURE ON THE LOCH'S NORTH SHORE.

THE SPICERS' TALE APPEARS IN THE LOCAL PRESS. OTHER SIGHTINGS ARE REPORTED. SOON THE STORY IS PICKED UP BY THE NATIONAL PRESS, INCLUDING THE DAILY MAIL IN LONDON...

WHAT DO YOU MAKE OF THIS LOCH NESS BUSINESS?

THERE COULD BE SOMETHING IN IT.

BUT IT WON'T BE REAL NEWS UNTIL SOMEONE GETS A PICTURE!

NOVEMBER 1933. A MAN NAMED HUGH GRAY IS WALKING BY THE LOCH, NEAR THE VILLAGE OF FOYERS, WHEN...

SPLASH!

WHAT ON EARTH IS THAT RACKET?

THE MONSTER!

MUST...HOLD IT...STEADY!

KERSPLOSH!

CLICK!

MR. GRAY TAKES FIVE PHOTOS, FOUR OF WHICH ARE **BLANK**. THE FIFTH SHOWS **SOMETHING**, BUT IT IS VERY **BLURRED**. THE PHOTO WAS EXAMINED BY THE MAIL.

IT'S INCONCLUSIVE AT BEST!

AND AT WORST, A **STRAIGHT HOAX!**

I THINK IT LOOKS A BIT LIKE A DOG CARRYING A STICK!

THE POINT IS, IF THERE **IS** A MONSTER OUT THERE, WE NEED TO TRACK IT DOWN!

DO WE KNOW ANY BIG GAME HUNTERS?

THE FAMOUS PROFESSIONAL HUNTER, MARMADUKE 'DUKE' WETHERALL, IS SENT TO LOCH NESS BY THE DAILY MAIL. HIS MISSION IS TO FIND ANY TRACE OF THE CREATURE.

DUKE DISCOVERS MYSTERIOUS TRACKS ON THE LOCH SHORE. **EXCITEMENT** RUNS HIGH. PLASTER CASTS ARE MADE AND SENT BACK TO LONDON FOR EXAMINATION.

THE MOULDS ARE IDENTIFIED. THEY BELONG TO THE RIGHT FOOT OF A **HIPPOPOTAMUS**, LIKE THOSE SOMETIMES USED FOR UMBRELLA STANDS. THE FOOTPRINTS ARE A **HOAX**. DUKE RETURNS TO LONDON EMBARRASSED.

TWO OF THE PHOTOS ARE USELESS. HOWEVER, THE THIRD SHOT IS SENT TO THE DAILY MAIL, OWNED BY LORD BEAVERBROOK.

LORD BEAVERBROOK, SIR!

IRREFUTABLE PROOF?

ALL WE KNOW ABOUT THE PHOTOGRAPHER IS THAT HE'S A LONDON-BASED SURGEON.

A RESPECTABLE PROFESSION, AT LEAST!

WHETHER IT'S REAL OR NOT MAKES NO DIFFERENCE...

...THIS MONSTER IS NOW BIG NEWS!

WHEN THE 'SURGEON'S PHOTO' IS PUBLISHED BY THE DAILY MAIL, IT CAUSES A SENSATION.

IN THE SUMMER OF 1934, REAL EFFORT IS MADE TO SOLVE THE MYSTERY. SIR EDWARD MOUNTAIN HIRES TWENTY-FOUR MEN AND POSTS THEM AT INTERVALS OF A KILOMETRE DOWN THE LENGTH OF THE LOCH.

EACH MAN HAS A PAIR OF BINOCULARS AND A CAMERA. THEY WILL CLOSELY OBSERVE THE LOCH FROM 8.00 A.M. TO 6.00 P.M. WHATEVER IS IN HERE, WE'LL FIND IT!

BUT TWO WEEKS LATER...

FIVE GRAINY PHOTOGRAPHS AND SIX METRES OF FILM - OF WHAT? DRIFTWOOD? A LARGE SEAL?

THEY SAY THE LOCH NEVER GIVES UP ITS DEAD...

...WHY SHOULD IT DELIVER US ITS MONSTER SO EASILY?

THE NEWS BECOMES DOMINATED BY THE APPROACH OF WORLD WAR TWO. FEW PEOPLE VISIT THE LOCH DURING THE WAR YEARS (1939-1945). THE MONSTER IS FORGOTTEN.

THEN, IN DECEMBER 1954, A FISHING BOAT NAMED RIVAL III IS TRAVELLING DOWN THE LOCH...

CAPTAIN, YOU MAY WANT TO TAKE A WEE LOOK AT THIS.

I'VE PICKED UP A STRANGE SIGNAL ON THE ECHO SOUNDER.

AT WHAT DEPTH?

AT 146 METRES, ABOUT 36 METRES FROM THE BOTTOM... AND IT'S MOVING.

GET THE SOUNDER CHECKED WHEN WE GET BACK TO PETERHEAD. IT MIGHT BE FAULTY.

THE EQUIPMENT IS FOUND TO BE IN PERFECT WORKING ORDER. THE ECHO TRACE CANNOT BE EXPLAINED.

BOOKS AND MAGAZINE ARTICLES ABOUT THE MYSTERY BEGIN TO APPEAR. THEY INSPIRE A NEW BREED OF MONSTER HUNTER TO JOURNEY TO LOCH NESS. THEY WERE DEDICATED INDIVIDUALS LIKE TIM DINSDALE, WHO TRAVELLED FROM SOUTHERN ENGLAND IN 1960.

Everybody's

The Day I Met the Loch Ness Monster!

ONLY ONE DAY LEFT OF MY TRIP! I HAVE TO RETURN WITH MORE THAN JUST FILM OF RIPPLES ON THE WATER.

VRRROOOOM!

OH NO! IT'S PADDLING AWAY!

I NEED TO GET CLOSER!

BRRRRRAHH!

SCREEEEECH!

NEARLY THERE!

BUT WHEN HE ARRIVES AT THE LAKESIDE...

GONE!

DINSDALE'S FILM CAUSES EXCITEMENT WHEN IT IS SHOWN ON BRITISH TELEVISION. HE RECEIVES MANY LETTERS FROM PEOPLE WITH SIMILAR STORIES, INCLUDING ONE FROM A MAN WHO CLAIMS TO HAVE RECENTLY SEEN THE MONSTER ON LAND.

PANORAMA

"MY NAME IS TORQUIL MCLEOD, AND MY SIGHTING OCCURRED JUST TWO WEEKS BEFORE YOU SHOT YOUR FILM..."

21

"I WAS TRAVELLING WITH MY FAMILY PAST THE LOCH TO FORT AUGUSTUS, WHEN I SAW SOMETHING MOVING ON THE FAR BANK."

QUICK! PASS ME MY BINOCULARS!

IT MUST BE 15 METRES LONG!

IT'S GOT FLIPPERS!

"IT WAGGLED ITS HEAD FROM SIDE TO SIDE AS IF IT WAS LOOKING AROUND..."

SPLOSH!

"...AND THEN IT WAS GONE."

MONSTER FEVER GRIPS BRITAIN ONCE MORE. THE MATTER IS EVEN RAISED IN PARLIAMENT.

THERE NEEDS TO BE A FLAT OUT ATTEMPT BY THIS GOVERNMENT TO FIND OUT WHAT IS IN THE LOCH!

IN 1961, THE BUREAU FOR INVESTIGATING THE LOCH NESS PHENOMENA IS FORMED.

IN OCTOBER 1961, AT THE INSTIGATION OF THE BUREAU, THE LOCH IS SWEPT BY POWERFUL SEARCHLIGHTS EVERY NIGHT FOR TWO WEEKS.

THERE! WHAT'S THAT?

CALM DOWN, IT'S JUST A STICK!

NOTHING IS FOUND.

DURING THE 1960s, AREAS OF THE LOCH ARE SCANNED USING SONAR EQUIPMENT. A PERMANENT WATCH STATION IS SET UP. MINI SUBMARINES EXPLORE THE DEPTHS, BUT THE EVIDENCE GATHERED PROVES NOTHING.

IN 1972, A TEAM OF AMERICAN INVESTIGATORS, LED BY DR. ROBERT RINES, OF THE BOSTON ACADEMY OF APPLIED SCIENCE, IS OBSERVING AT URQUHART BAY...

WHOA! CAN YOU SEE THAT?

UNBELIEVABLE! ROLL THE CAMERA! ROLL THE CAMERA!

FIRST TARGET IS 6 METRES FROM THE CAMERA!

WE'RE GOING TO GET A PICTURE!

LATER, IN THE DARKROOM...

THAT'S A FIN, ISN'T IT?

WE'LL KNOW MORE AFTER NASA ENHANCES THE PHOTOGRAPHS.

THE PICTURES ARE ENHANCED USING THE LATEST TECHNOLOGY. THEY APPEAR TO SHOW A FIVE-SIDED FLIPPER, AND GENERATE MASSIVE ATTENTION FROM THE MEDIA.

NATURALISTS SPECULATE ON THE POSSIBLE SPECIES OF THE CREATURE. MANY BELIEVE THE CREATURE IS A PLESIOSAUR, LONG-BELIEVED TO BE EXTINCT.

BUT NOT **EVERYONE** IS CONVINCED.

THE SMITHSONIAN INSTITUTION THINKS NESSIE IS REAL. WHAT IS **YOUR** COMMENT?

THE BRITISH NATURAL HISTORY MUSEUM HAS DECIDED THAT THE PHOTOGRAPHS DON'T SHOW ENOUGH TO ESTABLISH THE EXISTENCE OF A LARGE ANIMAL IN THE LOCH...

SO THE HUNT FOR NESSIE CONTINUES...

OCTOBER 9, 1987. OPERATION DEEPSCAN, THE LARGEST INVESTIGATION OF THE LOCH YET ATTEMPTED, GETS UNDERWAY. TWENTY-FOUR CRUISERS, EACH FITTED WITH A HIGH-TECH ECHO SOUNDER, SWEEP DOWN THE LOCH FROM THE FORT AUGUSTUS END.

FOLLOWING THEM IS A PURSUIT BOAT, FITTED WITH THE LATEST SCANNING SONAR, IT IS READY TO LOCK ON TO ANY TARGETS FOUND BY THE FLOTILLA. TV CREWS AND THE PUBLIC CROWD THE AREA. THE EYES OF THE WORLD ARE ON LOCH NESS.

SOON, THREE CONTACTS WITH AN OBJECT ARE CALLED IN BUT 'LOST' WHEN THE PURSUIT BOAT ARRIVES. BUT THEN...

IT IS AT A DEPTH OF 184 METRES.

IT MUST HAVE COME IN BEHIND THE OTHER BOATS!

TꞪE LAKE CꞪAMPLAIN MONSTER

FOUR HUNDRED YEARS AGO, AT A SACRED ABENAKI CAVE NEAR WHAT WOULD LATER BE KNOWN AS LAKE CHAMPLAIN, VERMONT...

COME! WE MUST SEE HOW THE CARVING PROGRESSES.

IT IS NEARLY READY, A FITTING TRIBUTE TO CHAOUSAROU...

...THE SERPENT OF THE LAKE!

33

JUNE 30, 1981. THE MANSI PHOTO IS FINALLY PUBLISHED IN THE NEW YORK TIMES AND CAUSES CONTROVERSY AMONGST CRYPTOZOOLOGISTS.

IN MY OPINION, THIS PHOTO MAKES THE BEST CASE YET FOR THE EXISTENCE OF A MONSTER IN LAKE CHAMPLAIN.

HOLD ON! DO WE REALLY KNOW WHAT **MADE THIS IMAGE**?

IT COULD BE A CAREFULLY CONSTRUCTED **HOAX**...

...OR AN UNUSUALLY SHAPED **TREE BRANCH** STUCK ON A SANDBAR.

BUT THE MANSI PHOTO CONTINUES TO DEFY RATIONAL EXPLANATION TO THIS DAY.

FOLLOWING THE PUBLICATION OF THE MANSI PHOTO, THERE IS A SERIES OF SIGHTINGS ACROSS THE LAKE. MORE SIGHTINGS OCCUR THROUGHOUT THE 1980S, AND INTO THE NEW MILLENNIUM. BUT THE REAL IDENTITY OF 'CHAMP' (AS THE MONSTER IS NOW NICKNAMED) **REMAINS A MYSTERY.**

THE END

SOUTH BAY BESSIE

The Lake Erie Monster

LAKE ERIE, OHIO, 1817. A SCHOONER IS SAILING 8 KM FROM SHORE.

LARGE OBJECT AHEAD! NORTH-NORTHEAST, AND HEADING OUR WAY!

WHAT IS IT?

CAN'T SAY! YOU NEED TO SEE FOR YOURSELF, CAPTAIN!

ALRIGHT, LET'S TAKE A LOOK.

1960: SANDUSKY FISHERMAN KEN GOLIC IS STATIONED AT HIS FAVORITE PIER, 11.00 P.M.

HUH? WHAT'S THAT NOISE?

SCRAPE! SCRAPE!

RATS!

SCRAM, YOU PESKY VARMINTS!

PHWUF!

HEH HEH, THAT'LL TEACH...

OH, LORDY! HEEEELLLLO!

PLIP!

KEN GOLIC'S SIGHTING CREATES A STIR. ANOTHER SIGHTING OF A SIMILAR CREATURE IS REPORTED IN 1969.

RYE BEACH, HURON, OHIO, 1983. JUST BEFORE DAWN AT THE HOUSE OF MARY LANDOLL.

MMMMM...LOOKS LIKE IT'S GOING TO BE A LOVELY MORNING...

...IS THAT A CAPSIZED BOAT? AND WHAT IS THAT NOISE?

SPLISH! SPLOSH!

OH, MY!

SMASH!

IT SEEMS TO BE PLAYING...AND LOOKS SO PREHISTORIC!!

NEAR VERMILION, OHIO, SUMMER 1985. BOATER TONY SCHILL REPORTS SEEING A WATER SERPENT.

ARE YOU SURE IT WASN'T ONE OF THESE?

LOOK, IT HAD FIVE HUMPS THAT CAME OUT OF THE WATER, NO WAY IT WAS A STURGEON!

42

LAKE BEASTS – FACT OR FICTION?

Before the existence of lake monsters can be proven, strong, reliable evidence must be found. But what kind of evidence do we need? Eyes can play tricks and photos can be altered to create deceiving 'evidence'.

What lies beneath the dark waters? Loch Ness keeps its secrets, for now...

GATHERING PROOF

Loch Ness is the only one of the monster lakes to have been thoroughly searched for traces of unusual lifeforms. So far, about sixty per cent of the Loch has been scanned by sonar. Sceptics say this alone proves there is no monster, but the steep stone sides of the loch and the temperature differences within, make it hard to get accurate scans. Until someone finds an actual animal, living or dead, the general view will always lean more toward doubt, than belief in the lake monsters.

Could a lake monster be a large otter or seal? Mistaken identification of ordinary animals has been put forward to explain many sightings.

SEEING ISN'T ALWAYS BELIEVING

Debris such as driftwood and unusual looking surface ripples can fool the eye into seeing things. Lighting and weather conditions can also play a part in confusing even the most reliable witnesses.

MONSTER FAKERS

Are some of the people who have reported seeing lake monsters telling lies? The Spicers in Loch Ness ran a nearby tourist hotel and had a lot to gain from newspaper coverage of the local area.

We also know that photos can be faked. An example is the famous photo of the Loch Ness Monster said to have been taken by Colonel Robert K. Wilson, a respectable London surgeon. It was widely believed to be authentic in 1934. But in 1993, it was revealed to be a photo of a homemade model attached to a toy submarine.

With a little know-how anyone can fake a monster photo. This is the famous 'surgeon's picture,' allegedly taken by Colonel Robert K.Wilson.

GLOSSARY

Abenaki A tribe of American Indians, who lived in modern-day New England and eastern Canada.

"alors!" A French exclamation used to express great surprise.

carcass The remains of an animal after the skin and flesh have been removed.

cryptozoologist A person who studies legendary animals that may or may not exist.

echo sounder A machine that produces sound waves to measure water depth.

enhance To improve.

extinct A species of plant or animal that no longer exists.

fault A fracture in Earth's crust.

hoax Something that is put forth as real, but is actually a fake.

inconclusive Unclear, indefinite.

instigation The starting of something, such as an investigation.

irrefutable When evidence is so strong that it cannot be denied.

flotilla A large group, usually called a fleet, of ships or boats.

"je ne sais pas" French phrase meaning "I don't know".

livestock A collective word for a group of farm animals.

loch A Scottish word meaning lake.

millennium A thousand years.

"mon dieu!" A French saying used to express surprise. In English it means "My God!"

"mon frère" French for "my brother", this phrase is used to show friendly affection between men.

obstruction An object that is in the way of something else.

"oui" French for "yes".

parliament Where laws are formulated, debated, and voted on.

phenomena A strange series of events.

plesiosaur A long-necked dinosaur that lived in water and whose limbs were paddle-shaped.

"regardez!" A polite way of saying "Look!" in French.

rustler A person who steals animals.

schooner A ship that has a main mast in the centre and a smaller one a short distance in front.

sonar A way of detecting objects in water using sound waves.

species A group of living things that share certain characteristics.

sturgeon A large bony fish.

surgeon A type of doctor who performs medical operations.

FOR MORE INFORMATION

FOR FURTHER READING
If you liked this book, you might also want to try:

Beastly Tales: Yeti, Bigfoot and the Loch Ness Monster
by Malcolm Yorke, DK 1998

The Loch Ness Monster
by Terri Sievert, Edge Books 2004

Bigfoot and Other Strange Beasts
by Rob Shone, Book House 2006

The Loch Ness Monster: The Evidence
by Steuart Campbell, Birlinn 2002

The Field Guide to Lake Monsters, Sea Serpents, and Other Mystery Denizens of the Deep
by Loren Coleman, Jeremy P Tarcher 2003

Rumors of Existence: Newly Discovered, Supposedly Extinct, and Unconfirmed Inhabitants of the Animal Kingdom
by Matthew Bille, Hancock House 1995

The Beasts that Hide from Man: Seeking the World's Last Undiscovered Animals
by Karl P.N Shuker, Paraview 2003

INDEX

Web Sites

Due to the changing nature of Internet links, the Salariya Book Company has developed an online list of Web sites related to the subject of this book. This site is updated regularly. Please use this link to access the list:

http://www.book-house.co.uk/grmy/loch